W9-DCD-461

postage
& handling

LEARNING

poems

TO

by

TALK

Robin S. Chapman

FIREWEED
PRESS

P. O. Box 482
Madison, WI 53701-0482

ACKNOWLEDGEMENTS

With thanks to the editors of the publications in which some of these poems first appeared:

Beloit Poetry Journal: "High School"
The Christian Science Monitor: "Pete"; "Vacant Lot"; "Learning to Talk"
Northeast: "My Father, the Sailor"
Poetry: "Catching Rabbits"
Shenandoah: "The Way of Your Going"
The Women's Review of Books: "For My Sister"

My thanks too, for the space and time provided by the Leighton Artist Colony, Banff, Canada; and the valuable advice of the Fireweed Poets' Collection and my manuscript groups.

The publication of this book is supported by a grant from the Wisconsin Arts Board with funds from the State of Wisconsin and the National Endowment for the Arts

Cover Photos by Sally Benforado

Printed for
FIREWEED PRESS
by
Inkwell Printers
202 E. Chapel Street
Dodgeville, Wisconsin 53533
USA

for my mother, my father
my sister Shelagh, my brother Kim

CONTENTS

Why is the Night Sky Dark?   7

I. THE BLACK BOWL
The Black Bowl   11
Lessons of Childhood   12
Hollyhocks   14
Mitten   15
Pete   16
Things We Remember, Things We Forget   17
Child's Play   19
First Names   20
Vacant Lot   21
What I Remember   22
Camp   23
Catching Rabbits   24
Books   25

II. THE BLUE GLASS
My Mother's Glass   29
Prefab   30
Maids   31
Boys   32
Rhinoceros Beetle   34
Sousaphone   36
Algebra II   37
High School   39
Boyfriends   40
Cabbages   41
DTs   42
Falsies   43
Thighs   44

III. LEARNING TO TALK

Learning to Talk	47
My Father's Books	48
My Father, the Sailor	50
For My Sister	51
Matching the Plaid	52
The Way of Your Going	54
Don't Call	55
Economies of Loss	57
Playhouse	58
Starting Over	59
Quilt	60
Holiday Phone Call	61
Summer Vacation	62
Gifts	63
Kim's Bear	64
Seventy-Fifth	66
Signs	69

WHY IS THE NIGHT SKY DARK?

I shall never believe that God
plays dice with the world.
A. Einstein

When our world turned its back
To the sun, those other stars far away
Did not rush to welcome us,
Though our eyes
Grew large as owls'
And we could make out
The actors in old stories.

Still many
That should have been there,
Flung like sand
Through the box of space,
Were absent, or jammed darkly together,
And we asked what we had done
To deserve this abandonment.

Believing in grace
And the ill-strewn stars,
Einstein deduced from these
A relativistic universe
And the weapons of nuclear war —
Pandora's box opened,
That old story,

Making theory of matter,
Though we've always known
Another answer — the sky fills
With dark because the sun
Has vanished, because one star
Is not the same as another
And the one closest to home
Is the one to which our eyes
Are tuned, whether or not
It returns. It is memory
That makes the night sky dark,
Our longing for what is gone.

I. THE BLACK BOWL

THE BLACK BOWL

It stood, low bowl,
On the mahogany bookshelf
My father had made,
Souvenir of Arizona trip
Of years before,
Where we'd stared at cliff cities,
Imagining children there
Sitting around
The smoky fires,
Leaning over ledges,
Climbing down ladders;
How did they manage
Not to fall?

One night
In the desert
We stared till sleep came
Into the only campfire
We'd see together,
Shivering
With happy cold
Under the black vault of sky,
Leaning into our parents' bodies,
Into the voices singing Clementine;
As the next day we'd hung onto their hands
Looking across an immense crater
Formed by a meteorite.

LESSONS OF CHILDHOOD

At two I stack blocks
In the playpen,
Knock them down again,
While my mother
Tends a fat white grub
Of a baby and a man
Who says he's my daddy
Has come and gone back to war,
A line drawn somewhere.
            Building, building I think.

At four I chant syllables
As this stranger, my father,
Speeds the car into morning
Where we will live, all four,
In a house with hammocks,
A quarter mile of wood-wolf noises
From the chatter of the settlement house
Where they will let me play baby;
"Baby Jesus maybe see us yay yay."
            Singing, I'm singing I say.

At five, I recite
To the assembled stuffed animals
From the dog-eared pages of my book
"And Muffin's family left him"
As we leave dog and home, drive
Through the gates of a city with guards,
Show the cards that say we will be allowed
To live among green Tennessee hills, briars,
And the mud of the gaseous diffusion plant.
I know every word of the story.
            Reading, I'm reading, I think.

At six, I leap for whoever will look
Through the sweeping
Arabesques and tour jetes
That Cinderella wept
Though my part's just the horse,
Stare from the stage
Into footlights and the dazzling black
Where my father and his friend
Clap; somewhere,
The sound of argument;
        Dancing, I'm dancing I say.

At seven I connect words
In an ode to a bee
We kept too long in an airless jar,
Rounding my letters like
Grownups in their notes to each other,
Putting my arm round my brother
To shut out the sounds
Of a howling new sister,
The hissing of fire over the dump,
My mother's crying in the nighttime house.
        Writing, I'm writing, I explain.

At eight, I work out on cards
Combinations of symbols I've seen
In physics journals
Now stacked with sawdust
And mahogany planks, machine saws,
Vises and clamps
In the deserted workshop room,
Thinking, if these were codes
Important enough to take my father away
They might bring him back;
        Algebra, I'm doing algebra, I say.

HOLLYHOCKS

I remember them tall over my head,
Fluted flowers, red and pink,
With their velvet throats,
Their yellow pistils like bright fingers,
The scratchy palms of their leaves,

And me, two, three? on the ground underneath,
Led off by older kids I barely knew
Who offered to show me something,
Asked to look;
I remember spreading my legs,
The hollyhocks overhead,
Cries of disgust
When their faces came close;
Then calls to supper,
Me lying alone in the hollyhocks,
Trying to see what was wrong with me.

MITTEN

Cherry red wool,
Color of cough syrup,
Rough comfort
At three;
Also the hole
In the thumb
My mother
Wanted
To fix.

"*I'll* do it!
I'll do it!"
I fought.
"Do it then!"
And the yarned needle
Flung,
Fumbling stitches and sobs
In the fight
We both won,
My mother holding as proof
The unwearable result,
Me with my clenched bare hands.

PETE

For two weeks Ria and I had tiptoed around
The mother cat's box, peering in whenever she
Would let us look, the dog's hot breath
At our backs.
                              And the kittens!
All heads, shut eyes bulging, the world
All fur, and mother's milk, and wriggling.
Not ours to touch till their eyes had opened.

We waited out the long hot days in our cotton
Pants, a year too young for undershirts,
Under the rain of the sprinkler, harnessed
Pete, the retriever, as horse in our sidewalk
Theatre, galloping to the rescue of the princesses –
Us too – shut up in the swing set's interior.

It was early, the day it happened, so early it still
Was cool, and grass heavily wet, and the road
Sharp with the smell of new tar: Ria banging
On my door, saying the kittens were gone. We searched
The house; Pete gone too, and his footprints
Back and forth on the floor.
                              Running and calling
Through the yards, we heard his bark; found him
Curled around four wriggling kittens climbing his legs,
Leaving a trail of tiny tar footprints, blinking
Their eyes, nuzzling his soft mouth.

THINGS WE REMEMBER, THINGS WE FORGET

At five I loved Dad, and Mac, the lifeguard
Who taught me the Dead Man's Float
After a winter of earaches and shots,
The stainless steel bars of hospital beds,
Echoing corridors, confusion of waking
Every four hours to figures in white
Bringing their long needles and thermometers,
The ache of a shot in the butt, jello
And cream of wheat, sleep, sometimes
Someone combing my hair and then
Mom and Dad standing there,
A voice saying 'visiting hour is over'
And the glass piggy bank that they left,
Dropping a nickel for every visit,
Clinking in a muffled, far-away way;
Sleep again, the stuffed blue clown
My only anchor to brother and home.

But at five-almost-six I forgot all this
In the deep water of beginner lessons,
The pure summer smell of chlorine, and Mac,
Who could dive and promised
That we could learn to live
In this blue and yielding element,
And, holding our breaths, we did,
Though I forgot Mac too,
In what happened next − my mother getting fat,
My father complaining his eggs were cold,
A baby sister coming home, my father gone.

Then I only remembered the dreams that recurred
Of living in jail, all us girls,

With gray bars, where we combed our hair
Prettily and waited for the men to come
Down the corridors, wearing their cowboy hats,
Holsters and guns — Roy Rogers, John Wayne —
And we held our breaths, as they stopped
At one cell or another, saying 'you' or 'you',
And opened, inexplicably, one or another door
On the lucky, chosen few.

CHILD'S PLAY

Sometimes we made altars with candles and drapes,
Ria and me on our knees and Ann the best she could,
The way we thought Catholics might do it,
Petitioning God or the Wizard of Oz
To make Ann's legs and arms whole,
Though, brittle and dwarfed, they broke
Dozens of times those years,
Including once when she fell off the couch.
Mother whispered her life might be short.

When stories were done we'd explore
The jungle of her mother's iris gardens
In wheelchair and safari hats;
Or parade down the street,
Ria in the lead with a cane, me on crutches,
Ann in her chair, and Harry,
Who laughed as we passed,
Got a good spanking.

Once we buried a puppet,
Dug him up a month later, to see how fast
You'd rot when you died; pretty fast,
It turned out.

But we were Dorothy, Ozma, Glinda the Good,
And pretend had nothing to do with real life;
It was Ria's mom who died,
And me who works with disabled kids,
Ann who became the minister.

FIRST NAMES

Ria's mom Alice was my mom's best friend,
Though I called her Mrs. Ruley then,
And could never call her any name at all
After she told me "call me Alice" —

That was just before she got sick
And had surgery, but it had spread,
So Ria's doctor dad got her male hormones
To slow it down and she grew a beard
And a deep voice and an eye popped out
And by then, we were almost through
With junior high and Ria had learned
To be mother to the three other kids,
And the last time I saw her mother,
When she said, "Be a friend to Ria and Ann,"
I could have called her Alice,
If I'd recognized her; but a few weeks later
She was dead, the first dead person
I ever knew; and a few months later,
Ria's dad wed, and Ria had time for horses.

VACANT LOT

Three long blocks down the town's Peach Road,
Past Pelham Circle and Pearl — how the names come back!
It was out of a six-year-old's neighborhood,
Three times as far as I'd ever wandered.
It was ragweed and goldenrod hot and sweet
And twice the height of the dog and me,
Exploring late summer territory — a maze
Of hollows and tracks, bindweed and morning glory.
I followed Pete, the dog, perhaps, and he his nose
Tracing the passage of possums and mice.

The day comes back in dreams or waking forty years later —
Nothing of my father's shouts or mother's tears
That must have sent me out of the house, or the knocking
On doors too early for Ria or Ann to be up,
But the smell of ragweed, wet in the morning,
The shine of spider webs, funneled and spoked,
The grasshopper big as my hand that spit brown juice,
The marbles, lost and nicked, I dug up and pocketed,
The pink in the throat of the blue morning glory,
The feel of the sun as the dog and I curled up
Easy in our weedy kingdom, dozing in the lap of the world.

WHAT I REMEMBER

What I remember is overhearing Mother
Say to Dottie, "He never touches me,
He's not even polite." And later me,
Sitting on the steps with Ria,
My friend, telling her something was wrong
With my mom and dad as I stared
At the spaced and close teeth of a blue comb.

Forty years later Dottie reminds me
How she'd come to visit her girlhood friend,
How Mother had given a party for her
And invited my dad, even though he'd moved out
Weeks before. How when the guests came,
He'd pulled me onto his lap to comb my hair,
The first time ever, and I'd hissed to her
"He doesn't do this when you're not here."

Though what I remember is a child on the steps,
Staring into the teeth of a blue comb.

CAMP

We lived in tents with wooden floors
And whispered ghost stories after dark,
Safe among the living trees
In the haze of clouds the mountains were named for.
Hourly bells rang our changes of station,
Rising to birdsong and the creek-fed shower,
Shivering back in the mildewed towels
To straighten the souring sleeping bags.
Kitchen duty or scrub latrines,
Archery practice or braiding gimp;
For all of us, the swimming lesson
In the mountain stream that stopped our breath,
Its cold reaching bone as the ripple of local water snake
Persuaded motion where before there'd been none.

I wrote home that I'd learned to swim and seen a bear,
That everyone helped with meals and cleanup,
That I'd spent a nickel to buy a tin cup;
That we'd sung songs around the campfire
And no, I wasn't homesick,
And would show them how to draw lots
For all the chores when I got back;

How could I say I wanted to stay there forever,
Among the green trees in the light-filled mist,
Bells tolling the changing of the hour
As though we were novitiates?

CATCHING RABBITS

Child in the southern summer
Stalking prey, I propped the flap
Of the army knapsack with a crooked stick,
Tucked inside the carrot that Bugs Bunny waved
Under Doc's nose every Saturday, hid
Myself in the briarpatch brush, ready to jerk
The string that would topple the trap shut;
Waited all that day, and the next,
For cartoon rabbits to come to the bait,
While, under the porch, the cat stashed
His halfeaten carcasses and, each night,
Rabbits cropped the blackberry shoots; why

Is this still important, that vision
Of the soft creature I would catch, befriend,
Stroking away the fright? And the damp heat,
The loud scold of the mockingbird,
The scratching thorns? I wanted
The knowledge I don't have yet,
Of how our two real lives might intersect

As the long week, later, I tried to care
For the fierce marsh bird, wings full of lead,
That I found in the storm sewer and brought home
To the tub, feeding him the only food
I could imagine, night crawlers wriggling
Through my fingers and down his craw. He lay
In my arms, twisting his head, the day he was
Dying, and I walked him out to see the trees
And the sky. I don't know yet what marsh birds
Eat, or how to repair their thin-boned wings,
Or if I could have saved him with such tutelage;
Now it's the child who teaches me.

BOOKS

I lived in them, shutting out
The loud house, far away
On an island
With Swiss Family Robinson,
Gathering breadfruit,
Lighting rescue fires;
Or setting the table
With orphaned Elizabeth
Whose maiden aunts
Didn't understand her.

At night I joined Heidi,
Lonely in town
For the attic room
And six pines
Of her Grandfather's mountain house,
Or became the mermaid
Making her choice
To love and drown,
The journeyer offering crusts
To the three-headed dog.

I was combing my hair
With sandalwood,
Second wife
In a pavilion of women,
When Mother came to tell me,
After two years of waiting,
My father was never coming home,
They'd fallen out of love;
Afterwards I kept reading
And put up my hair
To wait for my husband to come.

II. THE BLUE GLASS

MY MOTHER'S GLASS

Long after bedtime
We'd hear the soft sounds
Of footsteps, the refrigerator door,
Rattle of ice, murmur
Of water, a bottle refilling
The glass from Mexico,
Tall, thick, blue
As the Caribbean,
Hazed
With bubbles, the waves
In it swirling,
Turning away.

Her fingers
Could follow the curves
Over the edge
Into the interior,
Cool water dark
With the smoky gold
Of bourbon.

Ice clinked there
Like temple bells,
Calling her to evening ritual
Wrapped in her terry cloth robe,
Blue glass in one hand,
Mystery story in the other;
Glass that drew her
Down its turning blue depths
Into the long tunnel away from us.

PREFAB

Only ten thousand dollars
For a house of our own
And a lease on the land
At the west end of town,
And ours was special —
Top of the hill,
Four trees at its back,
And a bank of violets
That a bulldozer scraped off
The morning we moved in;
There was the lonely wonder
Of rooms of our own,
The smell of varnish,
Plaster, aluminum sash,
A combination kitchen
And dining room, with Mother's bed,
Combination washer-drier too,
That shook the dishes,
And an asphalt driveway
Running through crabgrass;
And Mother, in gardening scarf
At six a.m.,
Out planting roses
In the scraped subsoil
Around the telephone pole.

MAIDS

We had two. Ida, who lived
In Gamble Valley in a house
The army had built with tarpaper siding
And oiled paper windows that her husband
Had shot her through, blowing a hole
In her leg that wouldn't heal.
Ida, with the high cheekbones
Of a Cherokee woman, keeping us kids
In line with looks while Mom
Studied stenography to get a job
And made the police look for Ida's husband
Who was looking for Ida, so she moved.

Winifred took care of us next,
And her ex-husband had already found her
And bashed in one side of her face
So that it always seemed as if that side
Were crying, and Mom got a job teaching,
And Winifred stopped her vacuuming,
When we got home, to ask about school.
Winifred, who gave us an electric popcorn popper
Before she left and said she was sorry to go.

My sister was old enough then to be on her own
So we got a TV and cleaned our rooms
And watched Howdy Doody's triple ghosts
On a snowy set and ate bowls of popcorn
And now I wonder who took care
Of Ida and Winifred's children.

BOYS

Till Ria and Ann, my brother Kim
Was my best friend, but at five
We decided to ignore him,
Making a pact to live together
And never marry;

At six, Ria and I fed Harry Carper,
Who had a crush on her,
A milkshake made of soapsuds and mud
And we chased Ria's visiting cousin,
A boy of ten, around the neighborhood
For weeks that summer,
Calling "Show us your penis!"
To keep him running, till he showed us.

In second grade I liked to visit
Larry Harper's mother, who made clay boxes
With ceramic flowers, and on the bus, Jerry
Gave me a turquoise ring and tried to kiss me
While all the other kids laughed,
And my mother made me give the ring back.

In third my father left
And in fourth, I kicked Daryl
In the balls on the playground
Every chance I got and ran so fast
I never got caught
In the games
Where the boys chased the girls;

And when Lonnie Spillers,
Who was big for his age
And always in trouble,
Cursed me in fifth grade
And threw out the window
The wooden angel
I got an A on in art,
I wondered
If it was only what I deserved.

RHINOCEROS BEETLE

The summer my legs grew long
I discovered bugs — rolypolies
Under the flower pots, bagworms
On the arborvitae, the black
Widow in the basement. The Book
Of Insects laid them out, their curled
Segments and feet, sticky camouflaged
Cocoons, shiny red hourglass mark.

Coathanger net in one hand,
Chloroform jar in the other,
I pursued their bright cousins
The Lepidoptera, cabbage butterflies
Sulphuring the muddy paths, orange
Monarchs on the milkweed, look-alike
Viceroys; dried and pinned,
They lined my cigar boxes.

My grandfather showed me a Monarch
That would drink from my finger,
The proboscis slowly uncurling
And curling, its feet gripping
My fingers, its black legs rising
High and jointed; it lived
On his dining room curtain for weeks.

A summer later, discovering
Boys, I sat at dusk on the steps,
Watched them go by in their cars
And not stop or call out.
I remember
There on the porch, out
Of the old book's night-bound creatures,

Finding once
The great feathered antennae
And large-eyed wings of Cecropia;
The unfolding, honeydew green
Of the Luna moth;
And late, come to the light,
Armorplate and horn, dark shining jaws
Of the rhinoceros beetle,
Shell smooth as the shaven legs
Of the older girls, who stretched
Them out for boys to feel,
Slightly gritty with sand and salt;
Boys with forearms of vein and muscle
Feathered with hair.

And the girl who glistened
In evening's lamplit aura
Like the still, translucent shell
Left in the critical moment of molt
When wings and thorax alike emerge,
Soft as any unfolding Luna moth
Drying its wings on the door.

SOUSAPHONE

On Fridays, my brother stepped out of the house
Into that golden spiral of brass, settled
Its weight, highstepped onto the floodlit field
Playing louder than any sibling shouts
The brass boom, the four-note solo — became
Someone the world would listen to.

ALGEBRA II

Skeet Burris is plotting the arc
Of his basketball shots on the board
As Vince Swazey coaches the numbers;
"Where should you let go," Mrs. Laycock
Had asked, "for the perfect foul shot parabola?"

While in the back Karl Elza and Mark,
Who've worked through the book already,
Are figuring out a self-teaching text
That would let them finish trigonometry
In a month — then, Mrs. Laycock had promised,
They could do the calculus they wanted.

Jay Bowles, who found the homework
Too transparent to bother with, is hard at work
Calculating approximate interest tables
On short term loans to the rest of us,
Aiming to prove to Mrs. Laycock and Mark
That you don't need calculus;

While Penelope Schwind and I work out
The Cartesian version of the equation
For the length of a triangle's hypotenuse,
Seeing that you can translate geometry
Into algebra just like she said
And solve for the missing side or angle;

And Mrs. Laycock, who can teach anyone math,
Has set us the problems that catch us still —
How Skeet will become the basketball team's
Most valuable player, Vince will coach
Secret agents, Jay make millions
Till the savings and loans go bust,
Karl and Mark accelerate
Into their brief futures— and Penny,
In her European braids, and I, still work
At how the old puzzle of no father translates
Into each new framework of the world.

HIGH SCHOOL

What sticks in the mind
is the black slinky in physics,
the twang of its wave
traveling the hall — still,
who could believe
water didn't travel,
watching the waves reach the shore?

Or the formula for angular momentum,
forgotten, like the words
to the 45s we collected,
but its sense connected;

Or Mrs. McGhee in American History,
sitting on the table
chronicling the Civil War,
swinging her divorced legs
and letting us in on history's secret—
It's all in the pocketbook —
and now we believe her,

Though back then, spinning
slower and slower
to "Stardust Melody,"
feeling the wave's motion
traveling the body's wires,
we might have given her
an argument.

BOYFRIENDS

At sixteen I'd had one date
And stepped on his toes
When he kissed me goodnight
While my girlfriends Virginia and Peggy
Were going steady with Tommy and Walter
And discussed with the rest of us whether
It was better for a man to be long
Or big around, voting for the latter,

And meeting Joel, from New York,
A summer later, I sat bolt upright
In the woods and talked philosophy,
Though when he got enthusiastic
Explaining calculus,
His arm against mine
Was all that I could see.
By the time we kissed,
Three weeks later,
I thought that this might be enough;
A long night later,
Held in his arms,
Hardly touching,
I knew they'd been talking
Technicalities.

CABBAGES

Her knife cut the head
Into hemispheres,
Laid open the stem
Reporting the world.

"People never change,"
Said my mother,
Ironing a shirt,
Refilling her tumbler.

Coleslaw for lunch,
Sunday corned beef,
Cabbage soup,
Vinegar.

In my garden,
Outrageously spread,
Blooms the flower that's stripped
For the cabbage head.

DTs

How mild they were, after all
The skid row imagery;
Just my mother, the teacher,
In her hospital bed
Worrying over the gray cat
Only she could see
In the corner, instructing the boy
Who wasn't there
How to run the film projector,
And then the film running;
The gray shapes
Scurrying under the bed;

Persistent voices
Adjusting the intravenous flow,
Asking her
To repeat her name, the time, the place.

FALSIES

My mother strapped them on each morning,
Unharnessed them each night,
Foam rubber breasts with no nipples
Tucked into white cotton cups. They rode
Before her all day, serene and unchanging
Under sweaters and blouses, enlarging the chest
She described as 'flat' to a perfect 36,
And after my father left, no man
Was there to find out.

      It was worse,
Or better, for the pretty, high-breasted girl
In my high school class, dated once by every
Shoulder-padded boy on the football team
To confirm what the others had whispered;
Green Kleenex filled her figure out.
My sister and I knew we were doomed
To helper bras or socks.

      Velcro-ing in
My shoulder pads that make me
As broad-shouldered as my mother was
In the war, I think of her again; her small,
Perfectly formed breasts, dark nipples taut
In the cold of undress, suspended for all those years
Between the mouths of the babies we were
And the mouth of the lover she finally took,
Abandoning pretense at fifty-eight.

THIGHS

"Feel these!" my mother demanded,
Showing off three months of health-club cycling,
Seventeen summers of sidestroke,
Seventeen winters of leglifts,
To her flabby-thighed married daughter.

Three months later she married Bob,
Lived happily on in her own ever after,
Spading gardens, making toffee
For the lengthening Christmas list,

So these stories, that she'd wish
I never told— black bowl, blue glass—
I understand they're mine,
Not hers, from times
She'd long ago forgotten
In leglifts and lists,
Keeping the future in shape.

III. LEARNING TO TALK

LEARNING TO TALK

for my brother

In the years when the house was loud
With argument and tears we learned
To cast voices, ventriloquists for
The lambskin dog, the comedian clown,
Petey the father bear, that trio
Who traveled the world together,
Beat back armies, caged or killed
Monsters.
        When the three were retired
To the back of the closet, eyeless
And balding, dribbling stuffing,
Our voices faded and the house
Fell quiet, except for the rattle
Of the tin can telephone, "Can
You hear me?" before the string
Went slack, or "Do you read me?"
Over the static of the walkie talkies,
My room to your dirt cellar dugout.
Sometimes a penciled note, "Send message,"
Arrived on the Lionel train whose tracks
We laid down the hall, or in a mailbox,
Thirty years later, stacked in a pile
With bills and junk mail.
        You work
For the telephone company on cables of light,
On memory thin as soap bubble film; I study
The talk of children at play, still trying
To make out the answer, "Can you hear me?
Do you read me? Send message, over and out."

MY FATHER'S BOOKS

Each time we'd meet, me bleary-eyed
From 24 hours on the Southern train,
Heat, and dust, stopping off
On my way back to college
For lunch and two martinis
In a Washington restaurant,
I'd try to focus again

On the theory of the book,
That involved the Lorentz transformations
To prove that the laws of physics
Had counterparts in the psychological world,
And conversely the relativistic universe
Took its shapes from our limits to knowing;
Here my limits would be showing

And I'd listen again, trying to get
A little more straight
Of the book that, still, he's writing,
Having gotten to page 138,
Including a chapter on how making love
Is like making salad, because it's a general theory
In which everything turns out to be relevant.

It took me 20 more years and a divorce
To call him up and ask him to visit
And put my own topics on the table.
Why had he left Mom? How had he lived
All those years I hadn't seen him?
Why hadn't he written or visited?

And he brought me a book
In plain brown wrapper
Called *How to Find the Love of Your Life*
In Ninety Days through meeting hundreds
Of possible single persons for coffee,
And he told me the answers, how somehow Mom
Had felt like his mother,
How he'd stammered in school,
Spent his happiest summers building a canoe
And taking it down the Arkansas River;

How he'd followed the young wife of a military man
To Washington and any mention of us
Made her jealous, him guilty,
And when she'd taken another lover,
He'd tried to make it up to us,
Kim sailing, me Europe,
Shelagh a new stuffed animal every year.

MY FATHER, THE SAILOR

You slip out
The sea channel,
New-dredged
For the flow,
Running before the wind.

Spinnaker swelled
Red, black, and gold:
Red for life,
Black for death,
Gold for What the hell.

Spinnaker
Red as an aneurysm,
Black as surgeon's thread,
Gold as the sun
Stapling the sea's horizon.

All my life spent
Watching you
Sailing away,
Slipping the shore,
The sea gulls crying;
May the wind hold.

FOR MY SISTER

We are the two faces
Of our mother's grief:
Public and private,
The one who denies,
The other who cries.

We are the two companions
Of the long
Husbandless past:
Follower and leader,
Peacemaker, caretaker.

All the boys who
Didn't love you,
All the boys
I didn't love;
We never knew

Till she let us go,
Rising like two balloons,
The future never comes
Till you ask
It to.

MATCHING THE PLAID

for my mother

You took apart and remade
Your flapper gowns
In depression years
While your mother
Sewed drapes for a living
And your father
Looked after the house
And the whiskey.
You made your sister
Go to town
Girdled and gloved,
Paid for her schooling.

You married late,
Lost years to war,
Lost husband to city,
Why, you never told
Though we heard you crying.
You stitched through our childhood
What could be mended,
Recut hand-me-downs,
Stayed up matching the plaid
Of the old material, paid
For our lessons,
Taught school.

Married again,
You kept your friends,
Bought new clothes.
Now your grandsons bloom
In bright plaid shirts you made
And I cut and patch
These words to say
How you taught the difficult arts
Of matching the plaid,
Ripping it out,
Getting it right,
Even when making do.

THE WAY OF YOUR GOING
for my mother

Shelagh calls at 5 a.m. crying
And already it is too late for this hurry,
Up and piling shoes and clothes
Into my carry-on bag, lists of appointments

To cancel materialize in air, the fastest
Circuitous flight scheduled, gas
For the car, plastic money, too late
For anything, no funeral to be held,

No fuss, even as I talk my way
Into the Admiral's Club at O'Hare,
Charge call to say I'm coming, too late
To stop me, the autopsy's done;

High over Tennessee, the furnace yawns,
I recognize the blue haze of the hills,
Plumes from the power stacks
Point the prevailing winds,

The way of your going; by evening,
Fumbling with well-meaning friends' binoculars,
Even Halley's Comet is colored by you —
Hazy blur like a thumbprint in the starfield

Below the three in diagonal line;
I have managed to see it
The last chance in my lifetime.
Goodbye, I say. Goodbye.

DON'T CALL

for my mother

I look at the black phone, same rotary dial
As the one in your house. It would ring
Without answer now,

As it did all the year of your dying,
And only you knew, making Bob tell us
Don't call, so I didn't,

While you sat in your armchair, took Xanax,
And wept, breathing in, breathing out,
Listening to the thump and slump
Of the heart you wouldn't fix.

I dreamed this morning I called,
You came, for breakfast on the porch.
I hand-squeezed oranges, ground
Coffee beans, made corn muffins, set
Your wild cherry jam in a blue glass
On the bright cloth. Everything
Just as you'd like, and we talked,

Of what we hadn't spoken of before,
The time you went into the delivery room
Hoping to die, your father hours dead
And husband wanting out. My sister
You brought back who carried your pain,
Tried suicide at thirteen. A son
You couldn't help to read. Me shut up
In a book. How you didn't feel sorry
For yourself. The question of happiness,

How it comes into your life
When you least expect,
Greeting you at the door,
Setting an apple beside your hand,
A glass of cold water before you—
Like sunlight
Streaming through the window.

ECONOMIES OF LOSS

Six months past our mother's death, Shelagh and I
Divide our inheritance, sorting clothespiles and closets.
What to do with the small gilt pots that once held rouge?
The gold-colored cases, tarnished now,
With their mirrors and a suggestion of roses? The sandals
With Cuban heels, fashionable forty years ago?

We begin to understand that she threw nothing useful away,
Kept magazines she meant to read, buttons clipped from shirts,
Screws that had lost their objects, and those other objects,
Gilt and gold, and that had lost their threads of connection –
How could she let them go, a girl's inarticulate hopes
Of what might still arrive, an invitation to dance
On the streets of Paris, a messenger knocking on the door
With roses? We try again to pitch the lot, save
Shelagh's painting of a frog. The few letters
We sent. The hat I knitted for her in fifth grade.

PLAYHOUSE

I watched the man next door
Build a playhouse of wood for his daughter
The fall he was leaving her and her mother

And suddenly remembered the log cabin playhouse
In our Oak Ridge backyard where my brother
And his friends had been caught lighting fires
And knew that my father had tried
To say goodbye to us after all.

STARTING OVER

Thirty years later, divorced,
I tiptoe out of a house
Whose mortgage is newly my own
To slash the buckthorn and walnut brush
Out of the yews, haul skateboards
And tennis balls back to the porch,
Prune dogwoods to let in enough light
For early crocus and daffodils
In the overgrown landscape
We had let go, remembering roses —
Those roses that Mother planted
At six a.m., scraggly climbers
That never bloomed. They
Could bloom here, the deep red auburn
Of her hair, in the black gold
Of Wisconsin topsoil.

QUILT

This white border
For the lonely years,
This red silk
For the joy she took
In bed. This cross-stitch
For what hurt too much
To think about. This needle
For humor. This interlocking
Pattern for her friends.

I pull her around me
On winter nights,
Warmer than I've ever been.

HOLIDAY PHONE CALL

It was our semi-annual catch-up
On everyone's life, me divorced,
My stepdad widowed twice — half an hour
Of his grandkids, my kids,
SAT scores, colleges, whether either of us,
Alone these last four years, had a date.
Bob was telling me how, at seventy-six
He didn't want to go out
With anyone who'd go out with him
And had discovered the advantage
Of living alone — you could fart
As loud as you liked
Without disturbing someone;
And as for his cold, four more days
Of his doctor on vacation
Would cure him or kill him,
He didn't much care which,
The difference not being as great
As it had at forty-six, and I said
Well it's been nice talking to you,
And hung up quick, though
Thinking now, it wasn't death
That had scared me, but how
Neither of us had learned
A cure for loneliness.

SUMMER VACATION

I was hearing for the first time
from old family friends
how our mother, who'd loved these vacations best
when she was alive, had refrained from telling us
that her father – or was it her mother?
her mother's sister's husband? –
was a full-blooded Indian, 'miscegenation'
being a word in vogue then
like 'genogram' now, the same way
she'd refrained from talking about why
our dad left, and we hadn't asked,

so all weekend we told each other
everything we could remember –
how Mary included us kids
in cocktail hour games,
told us about my dad's other women,
took us skinnydipping
by flashlight. How Lyman
taught us to clam and crab
and hypnotize ourselves
and build campfires and hold knives.
How Lyman threw green apples
at Mary's other dates
and they married at eighteen,
pregnant. His parents, who
cut him off. Our mother,
who had liked to laugh,
and sang too far back in her throat.

GIFTS

Each of us has one.
Kim has a knack of opening locks.
Dad can see four leaf clovers.
I find bird feathers, even wings.
Shelagh picks up lost cat whiskers,
Keeps hundreds of them
In a vase in the hutch,
And her lovers learn from her
How to give up co-dependency
And say what they feel
And honor boundaries and marry
The next woman they meet
When they leave her,

And I stopped worrying for her
When I saw the cat whisker collection,
Figuring it would take some time
Before she'd meet an older soul than she.

KIM'S BEAR

Petey, the bear's name was, yellow and brown,
And he stood by my brother when Kim
Went out in a pinafore
And the neighborhood kids laughed him in.
Petey was the man of the family, the father
Who never left; he believed Kim was a wonderful kid,
And listened to all his stories, watched him
Take apart radios and solder his first Heath Kit.

Petey waited for Kim to come back from the summer
Sailing with the other father and smiled
On Kim's braces and Playboys and sousaphone practice
And karate lessons and rock band rehearsals
And girlfriend and comforted Kim
When he stepped on the gas instead of the brake
And drove the Ford's front end
Through the house's foundation and said
He was still a great person
Even if he couldn't learn Spanish,

And if Petey couldn't go off to college with Kim,
Still, a father has a right to proud of a son
Working his way through school, patenting inventions,
Struggling to make sense of his life, a son
Who loved him too.

At dinner this year, Kim tells
His daughter that his father figure was a stuffed bear,
And the only way he could get Mother's attention
Was to make her mad, and even that wasn't enough
To get my nose out of a book, and the reading he still
Has to fake, and she better call before staying out
All night again with a guy, and had she fallen in love?

And Erin said no, and he should talk, and Kim
Looked at her and said, "At least you're authentic"
And they grinned at each other, a daughter and a man
Who had learned to be a father
From a yellow and brown stuffed bear.

SEVENTY-FIFTH

For the second time in his life we gather
To celebrate my father's birthday — Shelagh, Kim and me,
In our forties, and him, and Shirley, not quite sixty,
Who accepted his proposal on Valentine's day.
Kim, on the couch, with a large green stuffed frog
On his lap, looks at our dad and says, "When I was a kid,
I felt like you rejected me," and Dad nods,
Dozing just a moment in the rocking chair
After being up till 3 the night before, and Kim
Pats Shirley, who's never met him before,
On the knee with the paw of the frog and says,
"I promised my support group I'd say that,"
And Shelagh, in golden hair and red dress
And crystal beads, brings in the carrot cake
She's baked in the candlelit house she made
The down payment on with the money Mom left her,
And we all stand up and put our arms around
Each other and sing with happiness to our father
And Shirley and Grace and Judy and our mother
Before her, our stepfather Bob, our half sister
And brother, our step brothers and sisters
Of four marriages on one side and two on the other,
To the stuffed frogs and bears and cats and dogs
Of our childhoods, to our kids and our ex's,
To each other and also ourselves.

SIGNS

She is taking her ghosts for a walk
Through the woods, the silent lover,
Absent father, angry brother, weeping mother,
The faces she has looked for everywhere,
Hoping to see her own.

Like the wind shaking the clusters
Of aspen and birch, questions pass
From one to another. Whispers rise
To a chorus, and waves, in counterpoint,
Swell and break on the lakeshore,

So that now, when she would gather them in,
To console and answer as best she can,
She finds them rooted there, white in the shade
Of hemlock and pine, taking their leave of her.

Instead, all day, the birds have come,
Chickadee, nuthatch, landing on trunks
Close by, as though there might be seed
In her empty hands, straw in her silver hair.